FATED IN WINTER

A TALON PACK ROMANCE

CARRIE ANN RYAN

FATED IN WINTER

A Talon Pack Romance
By Carrie Ann Ryan

Fated in Winter
A Talon Pack Romance
By: Carrie Ann Ryan
© 2021 Carrie Ann Ryan
eBook ISBN: 978-1-63695-226-0
Paperback ISBN: 978-1-63695-139-3

Cover Art by Sweet N Spicy Designs

For my readers.
Long Live The Pack!

"Count on Carrie Ann Ryan for emotional, sexy, character driven stories that capture your heart!" – Carly Phillips, NY Times bestselling author

"Carrie Ann Ryan's romances are my newest addiction! The emotion in her books captures me from the very beginning. The hope and healing hold me close until the end. These love stories will simply sweep you away." ~ NYT Bestselling Author Deveny Perry

"Carrie Ann Ryan writes the perfect balance of sweet and heat ensuring every story feeds the soul." - Audrey Carlan, #1 New York Times Bestselling Author

"Carrie Ann Ryan never fails to draw readers in with passion, raw sensuality, and characters that pop off the page. Any book by Carrie Ann is an absolute treat." – New York Times Bestselling Author J. Kenner

"Carrie Ann Ryan knows how to pull your heart-strings and make your pulse pound! Her wonderful Redwood Pack series will draw you in and keep you reading long into the night. I can't wait to see what comes next with the new generation, the Talons. Keep them coming, Carrie Ann!" –Lara Adrian, New York Times bestselling author of CRAVE THE NIGHT

"With snarky humor, sizzling love scenes, and brilliant, imaginative worldbuilding, The Dante's Circle series reads as if Carrie Ann Ryan peeked at my personal wish list!" – NYT Bestselling Author, Larissa Ione

"Carrie Ann Ryan writes sexy shifters in a world full of passionate happily-ever-afters." – *New York Times* Bestselling Author Vivian Arend

"Carrie Ann's books are sexy with characters you can't help but love from page one. They are heat and heart blended to perfection." *New York Times* Bestselling Author Jayne Rylon

Carrie Ann Ryan's books are wickedly funny and deliciously hot, with plenty of twists to keep you guessing. They'll keep you up all night!" USA Today Bestselling Author Cari Quinn

"Once again, Carrie Ann Ryan knocks the Dante's Circle series out of the park. The queen of hot, sexy, enthralling paranormal romance, Carrie Ann is an author not to miss!" *New York Times* bestselling Author Marie Harte

FATED IN WINTER

Conner Jamenson knows two things:

One day he might turn rogue.

And he can never risk his mate.

Romy Temple knows what it means to be lonely.

She's spent ninety-nine years in the Talon Pack, not part of the hierarchy, and not quite old enough to be elder.

She's the wolf no one remembers.

With a rogue on the loose and the winter season approaching, two wolves who promised they would never fall find themselves on the brink of doing what could cost them the most.

Each other.

CHAPTER 1

Conner

"I'M NOT DOING IT." I shook my head and stared off into the distance. "It just doesn't feel the same without her."

My brother Nico sighed heavily next to me and leaned further back onto the rock face. We sat at the edge of a cliff, our feet dangling but decently safe. We had been doing this since we were kids, both of our fathers coming to our rescue and teaching us exactly how to sit, as wolves and in our human form, and not fall to our deaths.

The Redwood Pack was located against a giant

rock face, the tallest peak of the den not quite as tall as Mount Hood, but close enough. When the sun shone, that flat edge of the face of the mountain sparkled and glowed and seemed otherworldly. It was the perfect match for a Pack of supernatural wolves.

Nico and I were near the top, at the flattest part where you could sit and perhaps even have a picnic, although no human in their right mind would make it up here.

The fact that my witch mother and nearly human dad had done so was more a testament to who they were and their love for my other father, who happened to be a wolf shifter, than anything else.

"She's mated. That's what you do. You find your mate. And if they're not in your Pack, sometimes you stay there."

"But she's a Redwood."

"Yes, she is a Redwood. She will always be a Redwood. But Kaylee is making decisions. She'll be back soon."

"This will just be our first holiday without her if she's not back in time." I knew I was grumbling, but my twin was the closest person to me.

Considering I had six siblings and three parents

in a loving triad relationship, there were many people in my life. I had over a dozen cousins, all of us having grown up together and still growing up together. Considering that wolves were long-lived and could live to a century or more, my parents and the rest of my aunts and uncles were probably not even done having children yet. Most just liked to have children all grouped together so that way their kids could grow up feeling like siblings rather than farther apart, but my mother had been mentioning how much she missed having babies in her arms.

Considering that my twin Kaylee was the first one to get mated, and had done so at a decently early age since we were only in our thirties, I didn't know if my mother had been talking about grandbabies or babies for herself.

I wasn't sure, and I would welcome another sibling, but no matter what they would never be as close as I was to my twin. We had a literal twin bond that connected us. It wrapped around the bonds we had to our Pack and to our Alpha.

All wolves were connected to their Alpha with a strong bond that could either be woven into the Pack bond itself or a separate entity, depending on what your wolf needed. My cousins, the Heir, Beta, Omega, Enforcer, and Healer, all had similar bonds to our Alpha, but the way they were connected to the Pack wasn't necessarily a bond, more like threads that wove together a giant web. At least that's how I had always pictured it.

I didn't have a connection to others like that. I was an enforcer, a lowercase E. It meant that I worked directly for my cousin Gina, the Enforcer, capital E. The moon goddess blessed her to be the one with heightened senses to the bond and her wolf in order to sense if there was an outside threat to the Pack. It was her job to protect our den and the Alpha. It was my job to ensure she had protection and helped her in everything that she did.

I wasn't chosen by the moon goddess, but by our Alpha. It was just how things worked. If I had wanted another job in the Pack, I could've worked towards it. I could've gotten a job outside of the Pack, made money that way, and helped the Pack blend into the human world that knew we existed even better. There was always a role and duty for each Pack member to make them feel as if they belonged. That was who we were. We were wolves. We were Pack.

Right then, I felt far too off kilter for my own good.

My twin had gone to Texas to find a lost Pack

member. She was a Tracker and had the same power that our father, Josh, did. They could see a photo or image of anyone in the world and search for them. It worked better with those you were fated to meet. At least, that's what they said.

Sometimes it was hard to imagine that fate could be real. Even though we were blessed by a moon goddess, much like other shifters—that we were just now learning about—were blessed by other goddesses.

It was hard to believe that there was a purpose in the rogues, in the ones that were so close to their wolf that they lost all accountability, all sense of who they were, and attacked without resistance.

It was horrifying and something I wanted to talk to my twin about.

Yes, I loved Nico, yes he was a steadying force in my life and in the lives of so many others, but he wasn't Kaylee.

"You're pouting. And a pouting wolf isn't an attractive wolf."

I flipped Nico off. "Fuck off."

"No, I'm not going to. Yes, you miss Kaylee. We all do. But she'll be back."

"And she'll be mated."

"Okay, now you're getting grossly grumbly."

I winced. "That's not what I meant."

"That's good, because you're getting creepy."

"I'm about to push you off this damn mountain."

"You could try. You may be strong, you may be the wolf that can shift faster than anyone else we know and without as much pain, but I still have tricks up my sleeve."

Considering our mother was a witch, Nico did indeed have some tricks up his sleeve. "You're wrong about the pain," I grumbled.

Nico frowned. "What?"

I hadn't meant to say that out loud, but since I had, and I was in a piss-poor mood, I shrugged.

"I have the same pain as you guys do. I just have it all at once. So it's excruciating. I can shift quickly, so there's that."

Nico blinked at me, then shoved at me. I gripped the ledge of the mountain and cursed.

"What the fuck, man? You trying to kill me?"

"Of course not. I would've caught you if you'd fallen. What the hell is wrong with you? Why didn't you say that you hurt? We all just assumed it didn't because it was so quick."

Shifting into a wolf wasn't a bright spark of white light and happiness. It twisted your tendons, broke your bones, and altered your body from one form to another. The laws of mass and thermodynamics did not work when it came to magic. Sometimes our bodies didn't want to listen to the magic and took it out on us painfully.

"Dad knows."

"And Father?"

Dad is Josh, Father is Reed, and Mom is Hannah. They were the original triad of the Redwood Pack. Since their bond had been created, more triads had formed in our Pack and our neighboring and friendly Pack, the Talons. Their bond had served to protect the Redwoods during our war with the Centrals. With each triad bond, our connection to the moon goddess, and to the powers that be, intensified. It was a good thing. It made things a little complicated when it came to figuring out who we were talking about when we meant Dad or Father because sometimes we still slipped up, but we always knew.

Reed, our father, was a strong wolf with a softer side. He tended to be a little more insular and focused on his art more than anything. Well, other than his family and his two loves of his life.

Nico and I had never lived in a world where we felt like we were anything less than who we were.

Our parents adored us, as did the rest of our family. We were blessed, and we knew it.

That didn't mean we didn't have hardships of our own, but they were different.

"You should've told me," Nico whispered.

"It felt like I was making up excuses for being as quick as I was. I never wanted to be that person."

"You're a good guy, Conner. I know you miss Kaylee because she's out there alone and could get hurt, but come on, what else is there? I hate that our sister isn't here. I want to wrap all of our sisters in cotton wool and protect them, but they won't let us. What's wrong, Conner?"

I shook my head. "I just want to protect her."

"And?"

"The twin bond helps," I muttered, the words tearing out of me.

Nico cursed under his breath, then squeezed the back of my neck hard. "Does it? Or are you using it as a crutch?"

"I don't know, Nico."

"You're not going to turn rogue, Conner. We're here for you."

"Yeah? Then why do I feel like my wolf is trying to tear off my skin more days than not?"

"Because you're a damn fine dominant wolf, and

it happens to the best of us. You have family here. Connections. You're not going to turn."

"And what happened to Darren? He turned on a dime. He has twin infants."

Nico shook his head. "He was a lone wolf before that, and sometimes you can't tell who's going to go rogue. None of us can."

"I don't know. My wolf is stronger than his." That's what kept me up at night and on edge—something that made the whole idea of going rogue more real.

"And when we find Darren, maybe we're going to be able to bring him back. He hasn't killed anyone yet. That counts for something."

"I don't know, Nico. I'm worried. There have been so many damn rogues recently."

I shivered as snow began to fall in earnest, and I looked out into the distance at the dark clouds. "We should head back in. Storm's coming. We shouldn't be caught up on this mountain ledge."

"Probably not. Mom would have our hide." He paused. "As for the rogue situation? You know the Alphas are on it. All of us are. We're going to figure it out."

"Maybe. It just seems like something's pushing more wolves towards that, and I don't know why."

"We will figure it out. We always do. But you have us. I promise you."

I looked at Nico and nodded before the hairs on the back of my neck stood on end.

"What is it?" Nico asked, before his eyes went gold. "Fuck. Darren."

Darren was a Packmate who had gone rogue four days ago. He had broken through the wards and left his infant daughters in their cribs, having not touched them, but hadn't alerted anybody else that he was going. That in itself was worrying, considering their mother and Darren's mate had been out at the time. It had been her first time with her family, just a moment so she could breathe.

And it had been the last time she had seen Darren.

He had turned without cause and nobody knew why. And now he was out hunting for something in the woods. The four Packs that made up this region and its vast territories were on the hunt for him, with no luck.

But it seemed that Darren had turned back.

"You got your phone?" I asked.

Nico shook his head.

"No, because it keeps going off and I wanted time."

"Fuck. Okay, can you get back down quickly? Alert the others?"

"And leave you with a fucking rogue?"

"I can handle it. I'm an enforcer."

"And what am I? Chopped liver?"

"You're a very fucking fast runner who's going to go get help. And next time, we will listen to our family and not leave without our fucking phones."

"Deal."

Nico gave me a gold-eyed look and then sprinted down the side of the mountain. He was fast. And I knew the only reason that he could move so far down a cliffside like he was doing was not just because of his wolf and agility, but because of the magic in his veins. Our mother was an earth witch, after all.

I pushed those thoughts from my mind and focused on the wolf coming at me. I could sense him, feel him along the bonds that told us we were Pack.

I cursed under my breath. I didn't want to kill Darren, but I also didn't want to be pushed off the side of the cliff. So I moved forward, distancing myself from the edge, and lowered my body to the ground.

I quickly stripped out of my clothes, knowing being in wolf form would be better for this. I could subdue him easier, mostly because I wouldn't have to be making so many defensive moves in my human skin. The shift was agony, bliss, and a sweet ending all in once. While others needed minutes in order to shift, to break those bones and alter their body and transform, I didn't. I needed moments.

I could shift back and forth pretty quickly, but only a few times. Much like any other wolf. And then I got exhausted and needed to sleep for hours while stuffing my face with food so I could replenish my energy.

I let out a slight chuff of pain as I finished the shift, left my clothes by the side of the cliff, and moved forward. I needed to pin Darren down, to knock him out, and hopefully we could turn him back. It didn't always work, sometimes they were too far gone, but Darren hadn't killed anyone as far as I knew. It had to be okay.

I hunted, following the sense, noticing not a single animal on the cliff's edge made a noise.

I kept moving, following Darren's scent, and twisted as a dark blur came at me. I rolled to the side and tackled Darren in wolf form. He clawed at me, and I pushed him back, spilling his blood slightly. I was faster, bigger, stronger, but I didn't want to hurt him. I just wanted to subdue him. I refused to kill this man. I did not want those two twins to lose their father, or for Darren's mate to lose him.

So I would do my best.

Darren lunged at me again and I shoved at his chest, snapping at his neck and trying to pin him down. Darren was smaller and wily. And, now that I recognized it, he was far too fucking smart for his own good.

I pushed at him again, annoyed that I'd gotten so close to the edge of the cliff. My feet scrambled off the edge, but I pushed forward, pinning Darren to the ground, then Darren bit me at the side, and I let out a howl, the coppery scent of my own blood hitting my nose.

At that moment, as his claws raked down my side and his fangs followed, I made a fatal mistake. My back paws slid off the side of the cliff, and I couldn't find purchase. I growled, and Darren scrambled back, his eyes losing their gold shine, and for a moment, I thought I saw the man behind the wolf, not a rogue.

Then Darren was gone, and I was falling. In an instant of pain and agony, I shifted back to human, knowing I could catch myself better in human form.

My hands clung to the side of the muddy dirt.

Snow was falling in earnest, and now ice was joining it.

My hands slid down the mud, unable to fully grip the edge of the cliff, and I knew that this could be it. I was falling off a cliff in the middle of the snow, naked. This was going to be how I died. Not by going rogue. By being a fucking idiot.

I nearly howled, cursing myself, and then a small hand reached forward and gripped my wrist.

I looked up into the most beautiful hazel eyes I had ever seen, and nearly fell in love.

"What the fuck do you think you're doing?"

At the sound of her voice, I knew it. I had fallen in love.

And whoever she was? She had just saved my naked ass.

CHAPTER 2

Romy

WITH A GRUNT, I pulled up the wolf who'd nearly jumped off the side of a cliff. I stepped back as all six-foot-five muscled man pulled himself up onto the ledge. A muscled naked man, and I did my best to keep my eyes on his strong jaw and green eyes and not any lower.

Instead, I looked over the cliff face where I'd just pulled him up from and shook my head. "Save me from boys who think with their dicks and not their heads."

The wolf snorted. "I'm a man. And I might think

with my dick sometimes, but I was trying to save it by shifting."

"And running it along a cliff face. Good job." I sighed, the reality of our situation settling in. "We lost Darren."

The wolf froze, his eyes narrowing. "He's dead?"

The pain in his eyes tore at me, and I wanted to reach out and console him. What the hell was wrong with me? "No. He got away. I had to stop my track to save your ass."

"Damn it. I need to find him." He let out a breath. "Thank you for the assist. I appreciate it. Now I need to get behind you to get my clothes."

My face heated up, and I moved to the right before my gaze tracked the bloody gashes on his side. "You're hurt." My wolf clawed at me, wanting to touch him, and I had to wonder what that was about.

He shrugged, wincing when it tugged on his skin. "I'll heal. Mom can do it, or our Healer."

I snapped my fingers when I realized why he looked so familiar. That had to be why my wolf wanted to be near him. "You're a triad kid."

"Got a problem with that?"

I frowned. "Of course not. I'm just remembering who you are."

He tilted his head at me. "And you're a Talon I

don't know, which is saying something considering I thought I knew everyone."

I knew why he didn't know me, but it was a long story. My wolf hid back, embarrassed. "I tend to stay on my own."

He blinked, studying my face as if trying to see into my soul. I wasn't sure I liked it, but my wolf did. "That makes sense. What's your name?"

"Romy."

"I'm Conner." He shook himself, then slid on his jeans, hiding his body, and my wolf whimpered.

This was so not the time. It never was. I was ninety-nine years old and would turn one hundred this Yule. I didn't know why my wolf was acting as if I'd never seen a naked man before.

"Where did Darren go?" Conner asked, and I met his gaze again.

"Into the woods. I've been tracking him for a few hours now; he keeps coming over the ward boundaries between the Redwoods and the Talons, but not towards the Centrals."

"Because they're such a new Pack, the wards are only bound with the moon goddess herself. It probably doesn't draw the wolf like it does ours."

"That makes me sense. It's just not easy. Was he your friend?"

"Is. He is my friend, as well as his two young pups and his mate."

I winced. "I'm sorry. I hope we find him. Without you going over the edge of a cliff again."

He shrugged, winced again, and I glared at the blood seeping through his t-shirt.

"You need to get that healed."

"I will."

"Are you just going to walk down the mountain with blood seeping from your side?"

"I won't have to." He lifted his chin, and the scent of wolf hit my nose. Nico, a wolf that I recognized, who looked so much like Conner that he had to be his brother, came forward, a few of the wolves at his side. Some Talons, some Redwoods.

"You okay?" Nico asked. He turned to me. "Hey, Romy."

"Hey. Your brother fell off a cliff. But it's fine."

"I told you you were going to fall off that fucking cliff," he growled, then his gaze caught the blood too. "What happened?"

We explained about Darren, and Nico cursed under his breath as a smaller man came forward. I recognized him as Mark, the Healer of the Redwood Pack. "Hi. Let's take care of this."

"I'm fine." Conner backed up, and Mark rolled

his eyes. "You know you need to get it healed. You know why."

They all met each other's gazes, and I caught the confusion as it ebbed in with mine, but didn't ask. Instead, I went to Quinn, a former member of the Talon Pack and now mate to the Enforcer of the Redwood Pack. "Hi there."

"You okay?" He asked, his voice gruff.

"I'm fine. I need to meet with the Betas, though, since both of them wanted to meet with me."

"You're going to be late then."

"Maybe, but I'm pissed off that I couldn't catch Darren."

Quinn reached out and squeezed my shoulder and then let go. Everybody was so awkward around me. Nobody knew who I was because, in the end, I didn't have a place.

I was a dominant wolf but in the middle of the Pack. I wasn't an Elder, though I was older than many of the wolves around me. I also wasn't part of the hierarchy, or friends with the newer wolves, because every single wolf of my generation had been killed.

All of them.

The Brentwoods, the wolves that held the mantle of the Talon Pack, like our Alpha, were all fifty to eighty years older than me. The others are much younger.

I was right at the age where every single wolf had died thanks to our former Alpha or the war with the Aspens or humans.

There had been so much loss, so much blood, that there was no coming back from that.

I looked over my shoulder at the foresty scent that was far too familiar already and met Conner's gaze. He tilted his head, studied me, and I turned my head away, breaking the connection.

I didn't know him, and I wasn't sure I wanted to. Everybody that I knew tended to die. It was hard to make connections when I was afraid that it would be the last time I saw them.

I pushed the thoughts from my head and followed Quinn back down the mountain.

The others followed, but I did my best not to pay attention to them. There was just something about Conner, and I wasn't sure I wanted to know what that something was.

We made our way past the Redwood bounds and jumped into the Jeep, Quinn driving towards the Talon den.

"Can you take me to the Central area, not the den, but the neutral grounds where we have the council meetings? Mitchell wanted to meet me there."

Mitchell was the Beta of the Talon Pack, and my superior.

"No problem. I'm off to go meet with Cameron about a few things."

Cameron was the Pack's Enforcer, and though he wasn't Quinn's higher up anymore, our Packs were so integrated thanks to our treaties, bonds, and matings, that it was as if we were one Pack with two sets of hierarchies. It worked because our wolves are the ones that make the decisions when it came to Pack dominance and hierarchy like that.

I wasn't sure if another set of Packs out in the world was like ours, and I didn't mind. I liked being unique.

I got out of the car, waved at Quinn, and knew I could jog back later if I needed to.

When I got into the building, keeping an eye out for anyone that could come at us, my shoulders relaxed at the sight of Mitchell.

Mitchell might be a mean son of a bitch, and a kick-ass Beta, but he also was a friend. At least a decent acquaintance. After all, people were good about staying away from me, so I wasn't truly their friend. Or maybe it's that I stayed away from them.

After all, I didn't want to be hurt. I didn't want to hurt others.

"Hey, you okay? I heard about the sighting."

I nodded, grabbed a water bottle from the fridge. "I'm okay. I lost Darren when I went to catch Conner from falling off the damn cliff."

Mitchell's eyes widened. "Are you guys okay?"

"We're fine, though I think Darren cut him up a bit. He shifted as he fell. I mean, Conner did. I've never seen anyone shift that fast in all my years."

Mitchell nodded. "Conner's the fastest shifter that I've ever seen. Might be the fastest ever. He can do it in a blink, and it's insane. He probably did that so he didn't fall to his death."

"That's what I figured, but it was still a little muddy from all the snow and he ended up sliding down a bit. I caught him by the wrist, but still."

"Well, I'm glad you were there for him." He looked down at his phone. "Nick should be here soon."

"So we're having a dual Beta's meeting for me?"

"You'll see," Mitchell said, and I frowned.

"I don't know if I like the sound of that."

"Well, you'll get used to it," Nick said as he came forward, a grin on his face.

Nick was the son of the Alpha of the Redwood Pack. That meant he was Conner's cousin.

There were honestly so many Jamensons and Brentwoods out there these days. It was hard to keep up.

"Your man here?"

"Since he decided to get cut up, he's back there. Our Healer healed him up, but he's off rotation for a couple of nights."

"I'm fine," a deep voice growled, and my eyes widened.

"What's going on?" I asked, stiffening. My wolf was at the forefront, alert because her Beta was there, a growl on his voice, and because of him.

Conner Jamenson.

What was it about him?

"Okay, let's get this over with."

I looked at Mitchell. "Is there something wrong? You have two wolves from different Packs here, ones that just were in a skirmish, and now both Betas of the Packs? I don't know if I like this."

"What she said," Conner growled.

"It's nothing bad. In fact, it's good, but it's a weird request."

My eyes widened as Conner met my gaze, and he shook his head.

Good, he was just as in the dark as I was.

"As you know, our Packs are a little different from others," Mitchell began, and Nick snorted.

Nick was young, even younger than Conner I thought, and he had so much power within him with the mantle of the Beta. The original Betas and Heirs and enforcers and everyone else in that hierarchy in the Redwoods were still around and still had connections to the Pack. But the Redwoods were so settled and peaceful that the moon goddess had blessed the next generation to give the older generation time to breathe. It was a great blessing to have that happen, rather than death or war, to create new leaders.

It meant that there was always someone there for advice, help, and to tend to the bonds.

The Talons didn't have that, but with the way that the Brentwoods were procreating and how we were settling into our foundations in peace with the Redwoods, I thought maybe in a few decades it could happen to us too.

"Anyway," Nick continued. "Yule is coming up, and we have never had a group event with both Packs to celebrate Yule and to thank the Alphas to show our support."

I blinked, tilting my head. "What does that have to do with us?"

"You'll see," Mitchell answered. "Our Alphas have had so much pressure put on them, even more so than any of us because they hold the mantle of every single bond of every single Packmate within our dens. And as Betas, our job is to take care of the Pack's needs. We ensure that every need of every single wolf is being met. And we haven't been doing that enough."

"Of course you have. You guys are just as exhausted as the Alphas are," Conner began, and I nodded.

"Exactly." I liked Conner that much better for noticing that and speaking up.

"Thanks," Mitchell said dryly. "We're working on it. It's why we have the Omegas and enforcers and everybody taking care of each other. But what we need is to show the Alphas that they did something right. And we don't want the burden to fall on the Alpha's mates like it has in the past."

I frowned. "What do you mean?"

"We are going to hold a Yule celebration. And you two are going to plan it," Mitchell said, and then grinned over at Nick.

I frowned. "Excuse me?"

"I'm not a party planner," Conner growled.

"Neither am I. I might be a woman, but I don't plan parties."

Nick threw his hands up in the air and pulled a five-dollar bill out of his pocket. He handed it over to Mitchell and cursed under his breath. "I thought that you would pull out the growly and sexism card later, but here we are."

Both Conner and I flipped off Nick in one motion and then grinned at each other. I pulled my gaze away, my wolf preening at the attention.

"What we're saying is our wolves are telling us that you two need to be part of this. And if it's the moon goddess saying that you two need a break and to be part of something bigger, then we're going to listen."

Mitchell let out a sigh. "So, to take care of our Alphas, to take care of our Packs, you two are going to be in charge of a joint Pack celebration for Yule. And you're going to enjoy it. Or I'm going to get growly."

I looked at my Beta and my gaze lowered instantly, my wolf clearly not as dominant as it needed to be. "Why us?" I whispered.

"You know why, Romy," Mitchell whispered, even though all the wolves in the room would be able to hear. I swallowed, my heart breaking.

"You know why as well," Nick mumbled, and Conner's shoulders dropped too.

I didn't know Conner, didn't know why he needed to be grounded within the Pack any more than I did. But I understood my reasons. I understood that everyone was worried.

Because people were going rogue, the balance was off, and those without pure connections and deep threads were leaving us.

And I had no one.

Conner, though, was surrounded by family. How could he have no one?

Our Betas had given us an order, and I wanted to give my Alpha something.

I didn't know any way out of it.

"Fine."

"Fine," Conner growled.

Nick and Mitchell grinned at each other and nodded tightly. "Happy Yule, let the festivities begin."

I looked at Conner and didn't feel festive.

It would be an interesting few weeks, and I had no idea what the hell I was doing.

CHAPTER 3

Conner

I STRETCHED my arms over my head and winced before I looked down at the claw marks on my side. Mark had done a good job healing them, but because of where they were located and the fact that they were claw wounds, he couldn't heal them completely. I wouldn't scar, and I wasn't going to die, but things still ached, and it was going to take a few days for the marks to go entirely away. So, every time I stretched, I tugged at the edges of the wounds.

I looked at myself in the mirror. My jeans were

unbuttoned since I had just gotten out of the shower, and my shirt was behind me on the bed.

I was off kilter. Kaylee wasn't here, and I had never spent this long away from my twin.

I hadn't realized I'd become such a codependent prick until she had been forced to go on a track to find our last Packmate.

Now I felt as if I couldn't function, and that wasn't a good thing. I loved my sister, but I needed to not growl whenever she was away because I couldn't protect her. She was an enforcer just like I was. She could defend herself, and probably better than I could protect her *and* me at the same time.

I needed to get over myself. But it was hard to do when all I could focus on was the fact that she wasn't here and my wolf was acting odd.

It wasn't that I was afraid of turning rogue just now, and while that was always in the back of my mind, because of how quickly I could shift and the way that my wolf reacted around others, that wasn't the reason I felt off kilter today. No, it all had to do with a certain wolf I had met the day before.

I didn't know this Romy. But I wanted to.

How could I not know who she was after spending so much time with the Talons? My cousins had mated into the Pack, and I spent more time with some of the Talons these days than I did with my own Pack. We were turning into one giant conglomerate of wolves, and I liked it. My wolf felt secure in that. And yet, I hadn't met her before. She scented new, and yet she had said she was nearly a century old. A century on this earth, and I had never met her.

It didn't seem possible. Although, the Packs were big enough, it made sense. I just would've thought someone who was on the trail of a rogue would be someone I knew.

And now it was someone I wanted to know.

She scented of cinnamon and honey, and I wanted to know who she was. My wolf clawed at me, not in aggression, but need.

Who was she? And why did I want her so much?

Something in the back of my mind whispered, but I couldn't quite tell what it said or what it was.

Was it because she was sexy as hell? Maybe. Or maybe it was because of something else? Something I couldn't quite name.

I shook my head, annoyed with myself, and moved to pull on my shirt. I was meeting with Romy later today, so I needed to get over whatever the hell was going on in my brain when it came to her and not act like a fool. I was usually good with women. I'd had dates before, I wasn't a monk, but it had been a while. Maybe my wolf was just telling me that I needed skin-to-skin contact.

Shifters were sexual beings. We liked skin-to-skin, and we enjoyed being with one another. Usually, sex could just be between friends to scratch that itch without the emotional complications that came with knowing that, while you may love someone, they weren't your forever.

Our wolves were always on the hunt for mates. Even if the human halves of ourselves weren't quite sure we were ready yet. My wolf wasn't sure what it wanted, and the human half sure as hell didn't want to give in. If I did give in, that meant I could hurt someone. What if I did turn rogue? The first person I would hurt would be my mate. I wouldn't mean to, but that's what would happen. So I would do my best not to be that person.

Not that I was sure I could actually hold myself back.

I had never met someone that my wolf was so intrigued with before, and that worried me.

I shook my head and pushed the thoughts out of my mind. There was no need to stress over something that wasn't going to happen. I had a party to plan. A fucking Yule party for the Alphas. And while I agreed the Alphas needed something, as did our Packs, I wasn't sure why I was the one that was supposed to do this. But it wasn't as if I had a choice.

I made my way outside and blinked as I saw Romy coming up. She had her dark hair piled on the top of her head, her long neck inviting.

I frowned. Inviting? Where the hell had that come from?

She had on a low-cut shirt that showed just a peek of cleavage every time she moved, as well as a wrap sweater that had a tie around her waist. She also wore dark leggings and thick boots that probably kept her legs warm and helped her with her footing.

Why the hell was I paying so much attention to the way that her curves filled out those leggings?

"I didn't know you were meeting me here," I said as I frowned at her outside of my front door.

She gave me a look. "I didn't realize I need your permission to be on your land?"

I sighed, my wolf not rising to the bait. After all, he was intrigued by her, and hell, so was the human half.

"I just meant I thought we were meeting at the neutral territory, not in front of my house."

She shrugged, the action forcing my gaze to her curves once again. I pulled my gaze up to those gray eyes of hers and swallowed hard. What was wrong with me, and why did she intrigue me so much?

"I was visiting Quinn and Gina, and since I was already in the den, I figured I would meet you here rather than where the council meets. As I don't have your phone number, it made it a little difficult to try to warn you."

I cursed under my breath and pulled my phone out of my back pocket. "I don't know why we didn't do that yesterday. I'm sorry."

"We had other things on our mind, like a party that we need to plan. And honestly, you don't need to apologize. I'm surprised you did."

I snorted, raised a brow. "Just because I'm a dominant male doesn't mean I don't know how to say I'm sorry."

"That's not what I'm used to, but I like it."

"Well, don't get used to it because I don't always act as I should."

She snorted. "Now that's the dominant male attitude I'm used to."

"Oh yeah? And a dominant female isn't the same way?"

"That is true. However, I'm not that high on the hierarchy. I'm not a submissive wolf, but you're far more dominant than me."

She met my gaze as she said it, and I found that odd. She was far more submissive than I was, but she was still a soldier. However, she shouldn't be able to meet my gaze for long. Maybe it was because we weren't fighting for dominance. Or perhaps it was something else.

And once again, I wasn't going to think about that. I wasn't sure I would like the answer if I asked the question.

"I was planning on doing a run around the perimeter before we have a chance to sit down. Do you want to join me?"

She looked at me then and nodded. "Are you still looking for Darren?" she asked, her voice a whisper. She was close to me now, and I wasn't even aware that I had moved, so I was a bare breath from her. My wolf reached out, wanting her, and damn it, that single thought I'd had in my head when I fell down that mountain hit me again. I wanted her. I had fallen in love with her at first sight, and it maybe had just been because of her strength, and perhaps it was just a joke in my head, but I knew who this woman was.

Damn it. She could be my mate.

Mate.

The word kept banging around in my head, and I

told myself not to worry about it because it was just a potential.

All shifters could find their mates. It might take a century. It might be the first moment that they start looking. It could be with humans, witches, or other shifters.

I used to think there were only wolf shifters out in the world, but it was recently revealed to our small group that there were cat shifters, and possibly other shifters out in the world, created by other goddesses.

The moon goddess had created wolves when she had seen a human hunter many eons ago hunt and aggressively attack a wolf for nothing more than sport.

She had been heartbroken and had forced the soul of the human to realize what he had done by merging it with the soul of the wolf.

From there, wolf shifters were born and spread all over the world. There are hundreds of Packs, all with their own histories and hierarchies and abilities to do much good and much terror in the world.

But with all of that, in order to create the new generation and to build upon a Pack, there were mates.

The one person who could be the other half of

your soul. Or third of your soul when it came to my parents and their triad.

You didn't have to follow your wolf's needs and desires when it came to creating a bond.

You could walk away. You could realize that there was someone else for you. The potential to mating was just that, a potential.

But my wolf was standing on alert, and he wanted the wolf in front of me.

And I wasn't sure how I felt about that.

Romy gave me an odd look, as if she could read my thoughts, and I truly didn't want her to. I could barely keep up with my own needs just then, and I couldn't focus, so I pushed all those ideas away. I would deal with it later. Or never. Maybe never.

And fuck, I just wanted to talk with Kaylee.

"Shall we go then?" she asked, studying my face.

"Yeah, sorry. Woolgathering."

"A wolf woolgathering, now that's an interesting thought."

I snorted. "How many wolves in sheep's clothing jokes do you think we get a year?" I asked, as we made our way through the forest.

"Probably not enough. We need more puns."

"That sounds about right."

I nodded at a few soldiers who walked past, and we made our way down the trail.

The Redwood Pack was located in the Pacific Northwest against that a face, but the Pack den itself was a series of homes and larger buildings amongst the trees. It was very nature-driven, and our entire goal with our den was to keep it eco-friendly. While the Pack was growing, we tried not to increase our environmental footprint. That meant we were on the front lines of ecological awareness. I loved the den. It smelled of earth, trees, and home.

Although far enough away, the Talon Pack was close enough that it was easy to visit every day. Our Packs were in the process of building a connection, a set of underground tunnels, to make it easier to connect the two Packs in case of war.

Through new technology and perseverance, our dens felt closer than they ever had before.

However, each den had its own set of wards. When the wards had been struck down during the war, all of our innocent had been vulnerable. But then, thanks to the sacrifice of some of my family members, and Romy's Pack members, the wards were back. They were magical in nature, and it meant that it forced those who didn't know the Pack existed to turn away and kept those who weren't invited in out.

"Did the wards just let you in? Or did Quinn?" I asked.

Romy blinked, and since I had realized we hadn't talked for a few minutes, she must've thought I was angry at her.

I cleared my throat. "Sorry, once again, wool-gathering."

"No, it's fine. And the wards just let me in. I did go through the sentry's area so that way they knew I was here, but the wards are magical, and just like you can easily go to the Talon den, I can come into the Redwood den."

"But like you, I always go through the gates, so that way people know I'm there."

"Exactly. It's not like the Talon Alpha can feel you through the bonds and tell where you are in the den."

"No, but I should ask my Uncle Kade if he can feel me if I'm in the Talon den."

"He probably can. Gideon said that he could feel us if we are far away, but he wasn't able to feel such long distances until Fallon came along."

Fallon was the Alpha's daughter and future Heir of the Pack.

My brows rose. "Really?"

"Really. We don't know why, but that little girl sure is special."

"And one day, she'll be your Alpha."

"Goddess willing," Romy whispered. "It'll be nice to have a female Alpha."

"The Aspens have a female Beta at least."

"That is true. It's odd to think that the Aspens are the ones that are ahead of the game versus us."

I laughed. "Well, with what they've gone through, they had to reorder their entire den."

"And all of the Jamesons and Brentwoods decided to have mostly boys, and so it makes sense that that's what the bloodline would reveal."

"We have more women though now. I mean, Gina is our Enforcer."

"I love Gina. She's so great. And perfect for Quinn."

"I didn't know you were friends with Quinn." I heard my tone and did my best to ignore it.

Romy gave me a look and rolled her eyes. "Not that way. I hated his ex-mate." She let out a little growl, and my wolf approved.

"I still can't believe she did what she did."

You did not break mating bonds. It could kill those around you, including children. Everything had worked out in the end, but Gina had almost lost her mate and future stepson in the process.

"Quinn and I worked together often, and I counted him as a friend. And then he moved to the Redwoods, and I don't get to see him as often."

"I'm sorry."

"It's okay."

"I still don't understand how I don't know you," I whispered.

"I tend to keep to myself, like I said." Romy shrugged as we moved along the ward edge, both of us on alert to scent for Darren.

"But you were at all the battles?"

"For most of them, others I stayed with the maternal dominants to take care of the children. I'm right at the border of submissive to dominant, where sometimes it might be easier for me to fight. Other times it's easier for me to defend. It just depends on my wolf and what she needs at the time." She looked at me then, a small smile creeping up her face. "That's not the case with you, I take it."

"I'm a little too growly for that."

"Well, it's good that the Redwoods have you." I sighed, and she met my gaze. "What was that sigh for?"

"No reason."

"Seriously?"

I shrugged. "I shift quickly," I said honestly, surprised I was even saying it. Then again, she was my potential mate, and she had no idea. Maybe my wolf just needed to speak.

"So you shift quickly. What does that mean?"

"That means I'm constantly on the edge of my wolf. Sometimes I don't know if that's a good thing or not."

We stopped then, and she turned to face me. "I think you have great control. I watched you shift, and it was a thing of beauty. Do the others know you're so worried about this?"

She was close to me then, so close all I had to do was reach out an inch and touch her. But I didn't.

I knew I couldn't.

"My family knows. My twin knows."

"Kaylee," Romy said with a grin.

"You know Kaylee?" I asked, narrowing my eyes.

"I do. So it's funny that you and I haven't met until now."

My wolf howled, wanting more. "Funny, that's one way to put it."

But before I could say anything, before she could do anything, a scent rose on the wind, and I turned. "Darren," I whispered.

"He was here, but it's fading. It isn't recent."

I cursed under my breath. "I don't want to go back to his mate and tell him he's dead."

"I don't know what I would do if I were to ever mate and lose them to being rogue."

Her words slashed over me. She could be my mate, and I couldn't tell her. I was one step from going rogue. I knew it. My family did. Everyone did.

I could never give in. I could never give into my wolf, to a bond, to anything that could hurt my future mate.

To anything that could hurt Romy.

And I hated myself just a little bit more that I was going to lose this potential after all.

Before I even had a chance to let myself go.

CHAPTER 4

Romy

"YOU'RE DOING WELL, Romy, but I hope you start meeting with the Redwoods more."

I looked up at Xavier and held back a sigh. I liked the Elder. He was a good man who always treated me with respect, but he also knew I didn't belong here. While the Elders were doing their best to reintegrate with the rest of the Talon Pack, they also had their sense of closeness, of reality. After all, they'd had hundreds of years together to form who they were and have their own language.

They practically had their own bonds, and

honestly, I wasn't sure if that was far off. After all, I wasn't going to know when it came to the Elders. Because I wasn't an Elder myself. Despite what I sometimes felt, at ninety-nine, I wasn't the oldest wolf out there. I wasn't even close. The Alpha was nearly a century older than me. And yet, sometimes, I felt like I had no one.

And that was a problem, wasn't it?

"I need to meet with the Redwood adviser today." Conner. His name was Conner, and yet I couldn't say it. I needed to just do so and stop having him take up real estate in my head. "We're planning a Yule event for the Alphas. Our goal, we think, is to make sure every person who wants to be part of the event has something to plan. Either with food, or art, or music. Anything that helps them help the Alpha."

Xavier grinned. "Good. Our Alpha pair need a break."

"They do. I just don't know why Conner and I are the ones that are in charge of it."

"I cannot speak for the Redwoods or Conner, but I can tell you that things are done like this for a reason."

"Again, I'm not sure why I would be that reason." I ducked my head, feeling more lonely than I had in a while.

"Romy, they wouldn't want you to feel like this."

My head shot up. "We don't know what they would have wanted because they're gone."

"Romy."

"No, I'm sorry. I can't do this." I stood up, and Xavier reached out and grabbed my hand.

"Romy."

The problem with long-lived wolves was that once we reached between twenty-five and thirty-five, we didn't age. Yes, Xavier was hundreds of years older than me, but he had not a single wrinkle on his face and looked the same age as me. But it was the eyes. It was always the eyes. Those eyes spoke of age, a past. Of a life long-lived.

Sometimes, when I looked in the mirror, I thought I saw something similar, but I wasn't sure if that was the case or me just trying to find something that was relatable.

Between our tyrannical Alpha before Gideon, the war with the humans, and the war with the Aspens, I had lost every wolf of my generation. Every friend, Packmate, brother, sister—everyone.

Every single person that had been in my circle, that had grown up with me, had died.

Yes, Quinn was close in age, but that was about it. No one else had survived.

How was I supposed to live with myself, to move on, when I had survived safely inside the wards when all of my friends had died?

I didn't even know how I could look at myself in the mirror, let alone find peace.

I hated myself, I knew I shouldn't, but I did. There was no coming back from that.

"Romy. Work with Conner. Remember that you are here for a reason. That we love you."

"But don't let the door hit you on the way out?" I asked as I sighed, shaking my head.

"You were important. You stayed behind the wards to protect the children. You are as close to a maternal dominant as we have, and you do so much for our Pack. I have lost many of my friends and family over the years. That's what comes from being an Elder, when you age out over the others. But you still have time, a whole world in front of you." He let out a breath. "I lost my mate long before you were born, my children too. I have to hope that there is something else for me out there, and that is why I'm here. To protect our den, to remember its history, and to ensure that our Alpha knows what came before us so we can look to a future of peace and prosperity. You have so much time in front of you. You are turning one hundred this year. One hundred years of protecting our Pack, of living. Don't look towards the next hundred as being a struggle, but as the potential to be who you can."

I nodded, tears filling my eyes before I let out a breath. "I need to go meet Conner. But thank you." I wiped my face. "I'm sorry you lost so much. I don't have words, Xavier."

"Romy. I am always here for you, but there are others for you as well. You don't need to hide yourself off in the Elder's part of the den to try to find your place. Everyone in this den wants to help each other. Remember that."

While I wanted that to be true, I didn't know if it was. Not when it didn't feel that way most of the time.

I gave him a tight nod, then I moved away, knowing I'd be meeting Conner soon. He was coming to the Talon Pack den this time, meeting with his cousin, Parker, who had just gotten back from Texas.

I knew a few things had happened down south with the Starlight Pack, but I wasn't quite sure what. It had to do with Conner's sister, but hopefully they would let everybody into the know soon if it was important.

And I wanted to know what mattered to Conner.

That put a hitch in my step, and I frowned. Why did I need to know about what had happened with Conner and his sister?

I didn't even know the man, but I wanted to.

I shook my head, and I moved down the pathway towards Parker's home. He lived there with his mates, Brandon and Avery, as well as their three children.

It was beautiful to see so many children born into the Talon Pack after so many years of it not happening. When the former Alpha had nearly destroyed the Pack, and broken so many natural laws, and hurt the moon goddess in the process, our Pack hadn't found any mates. It wasn't until Quinn and Gina that mating had even begun to happen again. And because of that, there was a gap in babies and matings. Now though, after peace had been found and our new hierarchy had proved that they wanted the good of the Pack and the Packs surrounding them, it was a baby boom. Everyone seemed to be having babies, twins, triplets. There was even a set of quadruplets.

We had a baby lion cub in the Pack, thanks to a lioness shifter being mated into the Pack. It was wonderful, so many little babies with their chubby cheeks and happy smiles.

We had lost so much in the wars and from our pain with the former Alpha, but we were thriving now.

And I had to remember that. That we needed to thrive.

Conner sat out on the front porch and handed me a soft drink as I came up. He nodded at me and gestured towards the cold icy glass bottle next to him. "Parker said you liked these."

I frowned and gave him a tight nod. "I do. I didn't realize he noticed that."

"Parker notices everything. So does Brandon, considering he's the Omega. I'm pretty sure between the two of them and Avery, they know everything."

I snorted but took the glass bottle with a slight smile on my face.

"I didn't think that anyone would notice that."

"They notice a lot of things, Romy."

Conner met my gaze, and I swallowed hard. "Oh. So, are they here?" I asked, changing the subject.

Conner shook his head. "No, they have the triplets out with one of my cousins."

"Another cousin?

"There are a lot of us. Now it seems there's going

to be even double the amount of Brentwoods. It's a little unnerving."

The thought of that much family, of a whole generation growing up together, warmed my heart, even as it made me slightly jealous. Or perhaps it wasn't that. Maybe it was just that I missed so many people. That I wanted everyone to have the life I didn't.

And when had I turned so melancholy?

Oh yes. When everyone had died, and I had survived.

"Why do you look like that?"

I blinked. "Excuse me?"

"What are you thinking about? You look like you're in pain."

I shook my head. "It's nothing.

"If you're sure," he whispered.

"Yes. Let's get to planning." I pulled out my tablet and brought up a list of things that Conner and I had gone over before. "We need to assign people to each of these without letting the Alphas in on it."

"We can do that. There's already a lot of people who've come at me in my Pack who want to volunteer."

I nodded, a small smile playing on my face.

"Same. People I hadn't even spoken to before all know that we're doing this without the Alpha knowing. So I'm pretty sure they're going to figure it out."

Conner leaned forward. "Even if they figure it out, they'll do their best at pretending they don't know. And that's not confusing at all."

I laughed. "Either way, we are going to figure this out together and assign everybody a part that they want."

"Sounds good to me," I said. "Okay, so food..."

We went through each of the things on our list, adding more as we went along. Before we knew it, we had dozens of people from both Packs assigned to certain things, and they would each have a team of their own using nearly everybody that we had talked to, and then some.

"This is going to be a little complicated."

"True, but I like puzzles."

I looked up at him, a smile playing on my face. "Really?

"Yes. I like the idea of fitting things into places and trying to make sure that everybody's involved."

I bit my lip, and Conner leaned forward. I could scent the forest on him, and I wanted to reach out, to nuzzle against him. My wolf sure was acting weird.

"Romy?"

"I'm glad we're not going to let anyone slip through the cracks."

I met his gaze, swallowed hard. "I don't celebrate Yule. You know, the Packs are just so big, and we've had issues, and so Yule hasn't been a major thing for me."

I hadn't meant to say the words, I hadn't meant to reveal any part of myself, but he frowned and set down his tablet.

"Maybe that's why they put us both on this." He let out a sigh. "Kaylee's the one that does most of the planning. She's the eldest daughter, while I'm the eldest son, so I usually just stand back and let her tell me what to do."

"I honestly didn't think you'd be the type to let anyone tell you what to do."

"You haven't met my sister." He paused. "Or you have, so you must get it."

"Oh, I do." I stretched out on the chair and then shook myself. "I need to take a walk. Do you mind?"

"Of course not."

We took our tablets with us, both of us going over other things, when Conner looked down at me. "Was there a reason we didn't meet at your place, but on the huge porch at my cousin's?"

I winced. "I have a tiny cabin in the woods. It's not great for meeting people."

He frowned. "Really?"

"I mean, I can show it to you, but I don't know, I don't invite anybody over." I paused, frowning as my words clicked. "I've never invited anybody over. How is that possible?" It made my stomach hurt to think about it, but I turned on the path towards my place. "Come on. We can change that." I needed to take Xavier's words to heart and try my best. All I could do was try.

"Are you sure? I don't want to step into your space."

"Conner, you're always in my space." Again I hadn't meant to say that.

"What do you mean?"

"You're just so big, dominant. You're in my space."

Conner seemed to shrink in on himself, and I could have kicked myself.

"That's not what I meant."

"Then what do you mean? I don't want to encroach." He paused where he was, not moving forward. We were behind a grouping of trees, no one around, and only a short distance from my cabin.

"Conner. You're very protective and dominant,

but not pushy. I thought you would be, but you aren't. I promise you're not doing anything wrong."

I reached out despite myself and gripped his hand. He looked down, threaded his fingers with mine. "Oh. Well then. That's good. You don't mind showing me your place?"

"No, I think I'm supposed to."

He raised his brows.

"I'm not good about letting people in. And as I was talking with the Elders today, maybe I should do better at not being that person."

"Then I'm honored." He moved forward, neither one of us speaking as we kept our hands threaded together.

I didn't even know what I was doing, why I felt the need to do this, but here I was, and there was no going back. We turned the corner, and there it was, my tiny little cabin surrounded by trees, plain, just for myself. I had built it after my last brother died, when I had nothing else. I made it from the leftover pieces of wood and lumber from the home that had burned down when the former Alpha killed my parents.

Sometimes I swore I could still hear their screaming if I listened hard enough. If I pressed my ear to the wood.

And wasn't that a cheery Yule thought.

"It smells of snow," I whisper, inhaling a deep breath.

"We're supposed to get another snowstorm soon. Actually, a few in a row."

"Today?"

"I'm not sure. I should probably check the weather."

His voice had gotten low, and I turned towards him, shaking my head. "What are we doing?" I asked, my wolf tugging at me.

"I don't know."

But he was the first person I had shown my place, the first person I had willingly let in my circle.

And there he was, still holding my hand.

And when he lowered his head, his gaze gold, I didn't stop him.

Instead, I went on my tiptoes and moaned as his lips pressed to mine.

CHAPTER 5

Conner

I HADN'T REALIZED I had cupped her face, hovering over her as my tongue delved into her mouth until it was almost too late. I couldn't breathe, couldn't do anything. All I could do was crave her.

This is a mistake, it didn't make any sense, and yet it was as if I was sitting in an abyss, wondering where I had been all this time.

Where Romy had been all this time.

And now there was no turning back. There was no going back.

Romy was here, in my arms, and she was kissing me back.

I wasn't sure what I was supposed to do or how I was supposed to breathe or how I was supposed to do anything.

All I could do was hold onto her, to kiss her, and to crave more.

I pulled away, knowing I needed to, knowing I needed to focus, and as I wrenched away, the two of us stared at one another, sucking in deep breaths.

"What was that?" she asked. She shook her head, ran her hands through her hair, making her look sex-tousled and sexy. "What was that?"

"Fuck. I'm sorry. I didn't know that you didn't want it, fuck."

"I'm not saying I didn't want that. I'm the one who kissed *you*. You didn't force anything, but why was that just so explosive? Why did it happen so quickly? I don't even know you, Conner, and yet it feels like I know every inch of you. Every ounce of your soul. Why is this?"

I swallowed hard, saying the one thing I shouldn't, the one thing I knew I was going to no matter what. "We both know why, Romy."

"How? I've lived nearly a century, and I never

thought I would find my mate, not after losing so many people."

I frowned. "In the wars?"

"I can't talk about it."

"Romy." I cupped her face again, running my thumb along her cheek. "Talk to me."

She pressed her lips together, her eyes looking as if she were fighting a war inside until she nearly exploded. "I've lost everyone. They're all dead. My entire generation. My family. They died in every war that we've had. I thought maybe my mate was one of them. Because I had lost everyone else, and it would only make sense that it's been so long that I must not be able to find my mate because they don't exist anymore. How could it be you? How are we just now finding one another?"

"I don't know, Romy. But I want to know. Is that wrong?"

"I don't know either. But we just met. And I can't focus. I need you to touch me, but I know I shouldn't."

"Are you as touch-starved as I am?"

She froze, blinking. "Why would you ask that?"

"I hold myself back. You know that. Because of the way that my wolf is. I haven't been with another person in too long, and you know shifters need that connection."

We needed sex, skin-to-skin contact. That was how our wolves survived—any shifter, for that matter, from what I had learned.

And yet, I didn't know if that was the case with Romy or not.

I didn't know if it should be the case.

"It's been a long time. Because of who I needed to be. Because of the things that happened. Maybe too long."

"But we can't blame this just on that. Should we?" I asked, not knowing what answer I wanted.

"I don't know, Conner. It's probably been far too long."

"Then it's dangerous."

"So we just see—the two of us. We just see. But no marking. No mating. I don't know you, Conner."

"You can't say this is just from being touched-starved. We both know that."

"Okay. Okay."

And then I kissed her again, and I couldn't think.

How could I ever think when I was alone with Romy? I knew from the moment that I saw her that she was something to me. That she could be something. That the potential there could change everything, but we couldn't do this. And we both knew that we needed to. That we desperately needed this.

Is this true? Is this what mating could be? Then again, mating had changed over time and was always different for each couple or triad. I didn't think mating could look or feel like this anymore. Not instant. It took time. It took moments of sensation and pain and agony until you could finally find that one person for you. It wasn't supposed to be an instant look of peace and knowing. It wasn't supposed to be a glance, and suddenly that was the person for you. At least, that's not how it had been recently. Not since the mating bonds had changed, since the moon goddess had been forced to make different decisions.

And yet, here we were, these choices, these decisions. And this was the person for me.

"I'm not ready for a bond. I'm not ready for what this could mean. I know this might hurt you, but I'm not ready," she whispered, cupping my face as I leaned toward her.

"I'm not either." I wasn't sure if I was ever going to be. But I couldn't tell her that, then again, maybe she saw it, maybe she already felt it.

Maybe that first sight didn't happen. It wasn't our first sight. It wasn't even our first touch. The first time I saw her, she had touched me. She had saved my life.

Maybe this was it? Maybe this is why our wolves were pushing so hard. My own wolf clawed at me to come in closer, but I had control. I had needed to have that control for so long because of who I was.

Maybe that this was this moment.

"Just us. Just to see. Just to touch."

"I can't deny that. I can't deny this."

"In my home? Or out here."

"I don't want to fuck you for the first time outside in the dirt."

Her eyes widened. "Oh?"

"Kiss me."

She did.

I growled into her, then reached around, gripped her ass, and lifted her up. She wrapped her legs around my waist, and I walked towards her house. The door was already unlocked, and we stumbled into the small one-bedroom open-concept area, feeling like a small gingerbread house to me.

I kissed her again and slowly made my way to the back bedroom.

"It's not much. But it's mine."

"And you're mine."

Her eyes widened. "Conner."

"At least for now. Right now."

I lowered her to the ground once we were inside her bedroom, the small double bed not big enough for the two of us. My brows raised.

She blushed, and I leaned down and kissed the tip of her nose. "I haven't needed much space."

"How long have you been hiding, Romy?" I asked, running my fingertips along her jaw.

"Enough that I don't think I can run or hide any longer."

"Then don't."

I had no idea what I was saying or what this meant, but I couldn't hold it back. It was as if this was meant to be, and this was who we should be. I kissed her harder, and then she was tugging on my shirt. I let her strip it off my body as she raked her nails down my skin.

"Claws, no fangs," I whispered, and she nodded, a smile on her face. "I'm not a submissive wolf, Conner."

"And I'm damn well not either."

And then I kissed her harder and bit her on the lip.

"Didn't you just say no fangs?" she asked, her eyes narrowed.

"Just human teeth. I promise."

Mating took two steps, two parts to lock into place for a bond to form that would irrevocably alter the two of us.

To complete the mating bond, you had to have sex, to join, that changed who we were together. That part would happen tonight, but the second part? The wolf needed to mark each other, bite into each other's flesh using their fangs and their human form, and mate mark them at the juncture of their neck to their shoulder.

We wouldn't do that tonight, even though I knew my claws, my fangs would elongate, needing release.

But not tonight.

And I knew the answer *should* be never. That I shouldn't risk her, and yet my wolf didn't care. It urged me on, nudging, and I would listen, just a little.

I pulled off her shirt, lowering my hands to her lace-covered breasts, and cupped them in my palms.

"You're so beautiful."

Romy snorted.

"You're just saying that because you want to be inside me."

My dick pressed against my zipper. "Well, that is true. You're fucking gorgeous," I whispered, kissing her again. My wolf wanted to bite, to mark, make her mine.

That was the problem with my wolf. I was always on edge. Always needing.

"Just touch, no bond," she whispered against me, and I nodded. Neither one of us was ready for that and I knew it, even though my wolf howled in rejection.

It wasn't rejection. It was common sense. Mating didn't happen this way, and I wasn't going to allow it. Instead, we kept our hands on one another, clawing at one another, needing one another.

I shoved off the rest of her clothes, her breasts falling into my palms as I undid her bra. She moaned, raking her claws down my back, and I let out a growl, kneading.

Her eyes glowed gold, just like mine did, and suddenly we were on one another, her claws tearing open my boxer briefs. She gripped me at the base of my dick, and I let out a breath, looking down at her. "Are you sure?"

"Stop asking. You know the answer." Then she leaned forward and gently bit at my chest.

"No marking." I remembered.

When she looked at the sting, she looked up at me and raised a brow. "I know. I need you."

"I've got you."

I picked her up at the hips again, flung her on the bed as she let out a laugh. That laugh did things to me. I could barely breathe.

This didn't make any sense, yet here we were, both of us trying to catch up. Our hands were all over one another, kissing and stroking and touching. And when I leaned down, slid my fingers between her legs, she moaned, arching into me.

"You're all sweet sexy curves and muscle."

"Talking about muscle," she whispered, clawing at my arms. I plunged two fingers deep inside her, and she was tight, wet, and all hot. My thumb went over her clit. She let out a deep gasp and came, clenching around my fingers with just that one stroke.

"Hot off the mark," I grumbled, and she slapped at my shoulder.

"It's been a while."

"How long?" I asked, needing to know. Being so possessive, I could barely control myself.

"Long enough."

I kissed her again, needing more.

I lowered myself further down the bed, pulled up her hips, and knelt between her legs. I latched onto her lips, pressing her pussy to my face as I licked, and I sucked, and I took in each moan of hers as if they were my due, my pleasure, my everything.

She tugged at my hair and I grinned, hummed along her clit. When she came again, I lowered myself to the bed, hovered over her, and pushed into her with one deep thrust. She clamped around my cock. I could barely hold it together.

"Conner," she whispered, her claws digging so deep into my back, I knew she would leave marks.

"Romy."

We froze, both of us connected as we tried to suck in our breath, the touch-starved tension that we had been in slowly receding into a temptation and addiction I hadn't known I had been craving.

I met her gaze then, and she arched her hips, letting me go even deeper. And when I couldn't hold back anymore, I moved.

We moved as one, me pounding into her as she met me thrust for thrust, and when she pushed at my shoulder, I growled, but I let her move me so I was on my back, and she was riding me.

I put both hands on her breasts, plucking at her nipples as she rode me, rolling her hips and sending me nearly over the edge. When she leaned down and kissed me, I slid one hand around her back, the other over her ass and between her cheeks to play with her, and when she moaned into me, bit at my lip, we moved faster.

My wolf growled, howling, needing more, needing to mate. To mark.

But I didn't. Neither one of us did. My fangs elongated, but I refuse to mark her. Instead, I kissed her, needing her taste, finding my addiction, finding my salvation.

And when I shouted her name, growling deep into her, I came, my dick twitching as I filled her. Her pussy clamped around me, her orgasm so beautiful I knew I would need to see it again and again until I found my purpose. My need.

And then the unthinkable happened. The bond snapped between us, a presence of warmth, peace, and beauty I'd never seen before. It was gold thread wrapped around gold thread, tightly wound between my wolf and hers, between the human half of my soul and hers.

She sat up, her hands going to her neck, and then mine, as we looked at one another, our bodies still quaking from orgasm, and we realized what had happened.

Without a mark, without the true force of our bond, we were mates. Bonded irrevocably and connected until the end of our days.

Our wolves had chosen for us without completing the mating in the usual way.

Tears fell from her eyes, and I sat up, holding her close, even as I was still buried balls deep inside her.

"Romy," I whispered, feeling as if I had found my other half, my purpose.

I could feel her loneliness, the way that her wolf reached out for any form of hope or connection. My wolf did the same, holding her wolf close, as if the two of us had never been near another. I wrapped my arms around her, held her close as she broke down.

"Romy."

"How?"

"I don't know. But I'm never letting you go."

This wasn't how mating was supposed to work. It was supposed to be a choice, a chance.

But her wolf had been so starved, and perhaps mine had too.

So the fates and the moon goddess had chosen for us.

My wolf ached, wanting to pursue and caress and to care for Romy until the end of our days.

Romy shrunk into herself, as if she were finally able to breathe, as if she'd been waiting for this her whole life.

I wasn't sure what would happen, who we would be, but I would never let her go.

The fates had chosen for us, and now I would learn to be the man I needed to be for this woman. For this wolf.

CHAPTER 6

Romy

I HAD BEEN BORN in another century. I knew times long ago, before the adults of today had taken their first breath, I knew of that time.

Therefore, I knew how mating was supposed to work. You found the potential for who your mate could possibly be, and through a dance, a courting of sorts, you decided whether or not to mate with that person. To create a bond that was so strong that it could change the very idea of who you thought you could be in reality, in life, and with that person.

In the century that I had lived, I never thought I would have that bond. Not when my generation had been wiped out through terror, war, torture, and hatred. My friends, family—everyone I had grown up with—had been completely wiped off the map. Some had been sacrificed. Some had given themselves in sacrifice in order to protect the Pack and the world.

Some had been taken by choice, some against their will.

Anyone I could have possibly found true happiness, a genuine connection with, had been killed before I'd even had a chance to allow my wolf to breathe. To take a step into that new direction and realize who I could be with those people.

I had never had a chance.

And yet, I knew how mating worked. You found that wolf, you slowly led yourself into that temptation, into that need, and perhaps, one day, the moon goddess would bless you, and you would know.

You would have sex, make love, create that connection in the first step of the bonding.

And then, as long as one of them was a shifter, that person would mark the other with their fangs. A gentle sensation of pain that twisted into a blissful agony.

That mark would be seen by others, but only for a short while. Then it would heal, and yet everyone would know that you were mated. They would sense that mark was still there.

I even knew other wolves, such as our Alpha, would continually mark their mate as a sign of possession. Possession that person wore with pride.

Our Alpha's mate, Brie, constantly wore outfits to show off her neck and shoulders, so she could show the world that she was proud to be mated to our Alpha.

She wore his brand, his mark, just like he wore the same mark on his shoulder and the scratch marks on his arms.

That was who we were. We were shifters. We were wolves. We were Pack.

One did not simply have uncontrollable, heated, best sex of your lives, and then get mated to another without a conscious choice.

But my wolf didn't look down at me with confusion.

Instead, she preened like a goddamn peacock and walked around as if she finally had what she had been looking for, for her entire fucking life.

My wolf had been starved.

And I hadn't even realized it.

I was mated to a Redwood. But I could still feel the bonds to my Talon.

I was mated to a man I didn't know, a man that I knew I could respect, but I didn't know how I could find the words to prove who I could be to him because I didn't know him.

I only knew his last name because I knew his family. Not because we spent any length of time together. I had saved his life, and in essence, this mating had saved mine.

And I hadn't even realized I was standing on the edge of the cliff, the edge of the abyss.

Conner may have fallen off that cliff, but I was the one who was still there, clinging for dear life.

And I hadn't even realized the floor had given way.

And yet Conner was there. His wolf was there.

And my wolf growled at me for thinking I could walk away.

She had made this choice. The goddess had made this choice.

And I couldn't think.

We stood in front of each other, both of us in our clothes once again, as we looked at one another inside my home.

My small home that I had created out of the broken pieces of my family home.

It was a shrine to all I'd had, and I hadn't even realized how morbid it was.

I couldn't truly hear their screams, and yet I told myself if I was close enough, maybe I would be able to. Maybe I could hear their voices. Maybe they weren't gone. Maybe the former Alpha before Gideon had finally saved us all, hadn't murdered my parents, hadn't butchered my family in front of me.

And I was a Yule baby. I was a miracle, and yet I couldn't believe in them. Not when everything was gone.

And yet, my mate stood in front of me, his eyes wide, gold, his wolf at the forefront.

Conner was just as surprised as me, and I couldn't even say a word to him.

I'm never letting you go.

Those were the words he had said to me as he had been buried deep inside me, both of us connected on a level far beyond sex and mating.

And yet, who was he?

"Romy?"

I pulled myself out of my self-pity and confusion and looked up at the man who was my mate. The man I didn't know.

"What happened?" I asked, my voice raw.

I could still taste him on my lips, feel his body on my skin. All I wanted to do was reach forward and rub myself on him, to mark him as mine and claim him as my own. But my wolf had already claimed him.

And I needed time to catch up with that.

I couldn't just throw myself at him and mark him and tell him that he was mine.

Even though he'd pretty much done the same to me just now.

"I need to go on a walk," I said suddenly, hating the way his eyes filled with pain.

"Okay." He let out a breath, stuck his hands in his jeans pockets. "I didn't know that was going to happen. I did not mark you by accident or anything. That was both of our wolves." He let out a shaky breath, then put his hand over his heart. "I can feel your wolf, Romy. I'm so sorry I didn't know you before this, but I didn't know you were hurting."

He could see all aspects of me. I had bared my soul before him, and I hadn't even known I wanted to. Or that I could.

And yet, it felt right. That I needed to.

Maybe this was why mating happened. That two

wolves needed each other so much it didn't matter what they, or the rest of the world, thought.

I need time to think. And I had to hope that he was strong enough to allow me.

I was more than an introvert. I liked my solitude. I reveled in it.

But had I choked my wolf in the process of taking care of the human half of me?

That idea scared me more than anything.

"I know you didn't, Conner." I let out a breath and did what I had wanted to do since we both pulled apart to get dressed. I moved forward, put my hands on his cheeks, and cupped his face. He let out a shaky breath and leaned into me, the stubble of his beard slightly rough against my palm. He smelled of home and everything I had been missing and hadn't even realized.

"I know, Conner. I didn't realize my wolf needed someone so much. I didn't realize anything. I'm really good at being alone." He pulled away, but I reached forward again, put my hands on his chest. "I don't know if I want to be alone anymore."

"We're mates, Romy. I don't think we're going to have a choice."

"No, I don't suppose we are." I let out a breath. "I

need to collect my thoughts, and then you and I will plan for the party, do all we said we would before. Make sure that each person in the Pack has the job that they want, then we'll find the rouge, and we will protect our Pack."

"And somehow, in all of that, we're going to figure out what the hell just happened?"

"Somehow. But do you mind? I need to walk."

"Okay. Frankly, I could use a moment to think."

"Are you going to call your twin?" I asked, not knowing I was going to say the words till they were already out.

He swallowed hard. "Yes. Though I have a feeling Kaylee might already know."

My eyes widen. "You have a twin bond?"

"I know not all twins do, but we do."

"I would like to get to know Kaylee better." I let out a breath. "And I would like to get to know you."

He reached out and brushed a tear from my cheek. I hadn't even realized I started crying. "I would like to get to know you, Romy. I can feel you along the mating bond, but it's so fragile I'm afraid to do anything more than brush against it."

"I don't think that either one of us is ready, Conner. But our wolves sure seemed to be."

"Perhaps. I'm still Redwood, Romy."

I nodded. "And I'm still Talon." I paused. "We both knew that the Packs were slowly becoming one, albeit with two Alphas. I guess that's truly a thing now."

"We'll have to meet with the Alphas and figure out what to do."

"There's a lot of things that we need to figure out."

I shook my head, went up to my toes, and did the one thing I knew I needed to do, despite the confusion and the uncertainty with everything else. I pressed my lips to his and kissed him.

He growled into me, a growl that sent shivers of sensation and need right down to my toes. I pulled away and swallowed hard, and he did the same.

"I'll call Kaylee and then meet with my Alpha. You go for your walk, but stay safe. And then we'll figure out what the hell is going on."

I nodded and watched him walk out of my tiny home, the home that wasn't anything other than a refuge from the outside world.

I looked around the place that didn't seem like the home of someone nearly a century old. Instead, it seemed like a shack out in the woods, the one with no memories and no connections.

How had I become this person? And how was I going to change that?

I shook my head and made my way out of my small cabin and through the woods.

I scented Gideon before I saw him, and that told me the Alpha had been upwind for a reason. He hadn't wanted to startle me. Gideon could hide better than most wolves than I knew.

He was one of the best, and he was Alpha for a reason.

"Romy?" Gideon asked as he came forward. His dark hair was pulled back from his face, his blue eyes startling against his skin. He was so dominant that I had to lower my gaze, unable to even look at him.

"Hi," I said, belatedly remembering I couldn't tell him why I was meeting with Conner. Of course, considering I smelled like him, and Gideon probably knew all about the mating bond, I had another reason for being near Conner. Not for the Yule and winter party that Gideon wasn't allowed to know anything about.

"I see congratulations are in order," Gideon said, and held open his arms.

My wolf shook in glee, and I swallowed hard before I practically threw myself at my Alpha. He caught me and crushed me in his hold. I let out of shaking sob, unaware that this is what I had been missing.

Contact, friends. My Alpha.

"Romy," he whispered. "It's okay."

"I don't know what's wrong with me," I said, crying into my Alpha's shirt. This felt wrong. This should be with Conner. And yet, this was also my Alpha, the man who might not be able to ever know me the way that Conner had the potential to, but my Alpha was the one that I should be able to trust without question. He was the one that I could rely on and lean on. Just like his family should have always been.

And that hadn't been the case. I had hidden from my Alpha and hadn't realized it till just now.

I had been hurting my wolf, keeping her from her Alpha, keeping her from the outside world.

And I couldn't do that anymore.

"You have mated," he whispered.

"I did."

"To a Redwood."

"You're mated to a Redwood as well," I said as I dried my face and looked up at him.

"She's a Talon now," he growled, though there was laughter in his eyes.

"You should tell her family that then."

"Touché. I feel you still in the Pack, but I don't feel Conner. It seems like the moon goddess is up to more of her shenanigans."

The fact that he could speak so easily and jokingly about a deity that he spoke to was awe-inspiring to me.

"I don't know what it means."

I told him about the rogue, how I saved Conner, and how we hadn't completed the mating, but the mating completed itself.

He frowned, but not at me. "We'll have to ask Xavier about that. It might not be that unheard of."

"I don't know. It's just, I thought I was supposed to have a choice."

"The moon goddess would only choose for you if she knew you would already make that choice to begin with."

"I don't know if I completely agree with that logic," I grumbled. "That's just an illogical fallacy."

"Or it's something that you needed?"

"I'm fine, Gideon."

"Are you?" he asked. He shook his head. "No, I'm going to answer that. You aren't fine. You haven't been for a while."

I took a step back, lowering my head.

"Don't hide from me, Romy. You are Pack. And we need to do better."

"What?" I asked, my gaze meeting his for a fraction of an instant before I lowered it again. His wolf was just so strong. He didn't even mean to do it, he was just Alpha, calmer, but he was a caring one, a nurturing one—exactly the opposite of his father.

His father, the man who had killed my family.

"We need to do better as Pack. Even in times of peace. Maybe even more so in times of peace. Our wolves are slipping through the cracks, and maybe we're doing better than we used to, but we aren't perfect. We need to do better."

"It's fine, Gideon."

"It's not. What will make it so?"

He looked over my shoulder, a smile playing on his face. "If we don't do a better job, I may have to deal with a certain dominant wolf."

I knew Conner was behind me. I had felt him on along the bond the entire time.

He had left, but he hadn't been far.

"I was meeting with Kade," Gideon whispered. "So we felt the bond happen between you and went to investigate it ourselves."

I turned to see Conner and his uncle, the Alpha of the Redwood Pack, come forward. I could see the family resemblance in them slightly, but Kade was no Conner.

And how could I understand that so quickly?

"I would say welcome to the Pack, but it seems like our goddess decided to make things a little more complicated for all of us," Kade said as he nodded at me. "Congratulations on your mating."

I blushed and lowered my head, letting out a breath before I rolled my shoulders back. I was a dominant wolf. The least dominant of this group, but still dominant. I needed to do better at this.

"I think the words I'm looking for are thank you, but it hasn't settled in yet."

"It will," Conner growled, and I raised a brow as both Alphas threw their heads back and laughed.

"Come on, Kade, let's go, give these lovebirds some privacy."

"I can go with you and needle you to make sure that your Pack treats Conner right."

"As long as we treat Romy right."

"Considering all of our family is so intermated at this point, does it matter?" Kade asked as he gave me a wink, and the two Alphas walked away, leaving me alone with my mate.

"How did this happen?" I whispered.

"You keep asking that, yet I don't have answers.

Are you mad about the mating?" Conner asked, his voice soft.

My wolf clawed at me, annoyed that we would dare hurt our mate even with that question. I went to my toes and kissed him softly. "No. I'm sorry for leaving. For needing that walk. To breathe. I'm used to just doing things on my own."

Conner tilted his head, looked at me before he pushed my hair behind my ear. "I guess I'm the same way. I'm so afraid that my wolf is going to go rogue just like the others, because of its strength, that I've been good at keeping my distance."

"I can feel your wolf across the bond. We'll never let you go rogue, Conner."

That was a vow I planned to keep. Even though I might not ever have that choice, I was going to prove to Conner that he was strong enough. That I was strong enough.

"Maybe my wolf needed this as much as yours did."

"As in, I wasn't the only one starved?" I asked, my voice low.

"I suppose not."

He lowered his head, brushed his lips against mine, and my wolf howled, feeling immediately like we had finally found what we'd been looking for.

I kissed him again before I froze and let out a growl.

My claws dug into Conner's hips slightly before I pushed him to the ground, and both of us fell, the furred body flying above where we had just stood.

CHAPTER 7

Conner

ROMY and I rolled to the side, both of us going to our feet as we moved out of the way of Darren's claws. The other wolf shook, his eyes bright gold with a manic emotion, glaring at us.

"Don't you let him kill you," Romy growled, and I held back a snarl and a smile. I was fighting by my mate's side. And the way that she moved, the flowing way that she was able to duck out of Darren's lunge, nearly sent me over the edge.

She was beautiful.

She had a grace to her fighting rather than the brute force that I usually used.

It would be a wonder to watch her grow, even more, to see the way that she fought and protected our Packs.

I ducked out of the way of Darren's claws and held back a growl.

"Darren, come back. You don't need to do this." I looked at the man who was a father of twins, the mate of a loving woman, and I didn't want to kill him today. I wanted to find a way to bring him back. Something was pushing these rogues over the precipice. Something was changing them at a remarkably higher rate than ever before.

I needed to find out what it was. I needed to protect my Pack.

But I didn't want to kill a man I could one day call a friend.

I couldn't.

Romy cursed under her breath, and my wolf pushed at me, feeling her wolf along the bond. She was so strong, elegant. She might not be as dominant as I was, but she was a brilliantly dominant wolf in her own right.

She was a protector, even though nobody had protected her when it had mattered most.

But now I would. That was my duty, my purpose.

I would not allow myself to become what Darren was, nor would I allow Romy to get hurt in the process.

She was my salvation, and I hadn't even asked for her.

I surely hadn't expected her.

I could sense other Talons coming near us, but at the same time, snow began to fall in earnest. The blizzard that had been threatening for days now had finally arrived, and the snowfall started to make it difficult to see. White filled my vision, even as I tried to sense where Darren was coming from. We were interspersed among the trees, the foliage so thick it was almost dark with the snow coming quickly. Cold seeped into my bones, even as Darren came at us.

The only reason that we hadn't taken him down yet was because there hadn't been a safe way to do it. In order to do it, we might have had to kill him. We couldn't do that. Not yet. There had to be a way to save him.

And that meant being careful.

That meant not being able to subdue him until it might be too late.

Because rogue wolves held extra strength that

wasn't normally theirs. It made them stronger than most wolves, even some Alphas. It made them deadlier, without remorse, without anything.

That meant sometimes it took more than a single wolf to fight a rogue. Even if that wolf was the most dominant of them.

"The storm's intensifying. We need to stop him and get covered," Romy called out.

I nodded, even though she couldn't see me, and growled.

"Darren!"

"Subdue him!" she called out, from the other side of the slight clearing we were in. I couldn't see her, the storm raging around us. The ice chilled my bones, and I jumped at Darren, only I moved too late. Darren twisted, and I growled, letting out a howl as Romy hit the ground, a high-pitched sound erupting from her mouth.

I growled low, reaching for Darren, but I couldn't find him. It was pitch black, the storm turning to ice. This didn't feel like a natural storm, but what did I know anymore? Everything kept changing, turning on a dime, and I needed to know that my mate was safe. "I'm fine," she yelled out, but I didn't believe her, not when she was so used to taking care of herself. Darren jumped, bit down onto my hip, and I growled, a hiss of pain escaping from my mouth. I'd been so focused on Romy, ensuring that she was okay, that I had been lazy. I hadn't been paying attention. My own wolf tore jagged claws through me, wanting to push forward, wanting to attack and to kill.

But that was my dominance talking, the strength of my wolf. That was what could turn me rogue, so I calmed myself, and I pulled on the bond that connected me to the one woman that could change everything.

"Romy," I growled again, but Darren twisted, digging his fangs into my side. Blood spurted, dribbling from my mouth, and I pushed at the rogue wolf, knowing that it might be too late. Knowing that I might not be able to save him. Or myself.

Romy let out a howl and jumped on top of us, wrapping her arms around Darren's throat. She shoved him off me as blood pooled, crimson in the whiteness of the snow, and we all fell to the ground, Romy holding the wolf towards her, as I crawled through the broken shards of pain that escaped over my side, and I held Darren down with her, keeping his jaws away from Romy's slender throat.

"I'm fine," she whispered, as we pinned Darren to the ground. He wiggled, thrashed, and I looked into her eyes, and then both of us looked down into Darren's. The gold shone brightly before it began to dim, not with death but with sanity.

My own wolf let out a howl, and even as the blood poured from my side, I held on to my mate and to Darren and let out a shaky breath.

"He'll be okay," she whispered, and I had to hope that that was the truth.

I leaned forward, kissed her hard on the mouth, and she raised a brow. "Is this really the time?"

"You almost died."

"You're the one currently bleeding out. So save me from that excuse."

She growled at me, and I couldn't help the grin.

The snow began to fall harder as I shivered and held Darren down along with my mate. When the others came through the trees, all on alert, with our Healer at their side, I let out a breath. The Redwoods must have been on Patrol near the Talon border and I would forever be grateful.

"I'm here," Mark said, a coat over his shoulders.

"Good, help my mate."

"I'm fine. Help your Packmate and Darren because my mate is the one bleeding."

"I've got it," Mark said as he came to my side.

Gina was there, taking Darren into her arms as Kade came through, his body sweat-slick from the run.

"Gideon's on his way. Are you okay?

"I'll be fine."

"If someone could help him stop bleeding, that would be great," Romy said, glaring at me.

I smiled wide and looked at my mate. "My mate is worried about me."

"Stop with the bragging," Kade said as he checked out my wound. "Your parents are going to kill me."

"Maybe, but I think my mate will be the one that does it first if I don't get better."

"Your mate," Kade whispered and shook his head. "Darren will be okay. I feel him along the bonds." He whispered the words, and I knew they were for me. Because I had been so afraid of going rogue, but Darren will be fine, hopefully. Somehow. He would be okay.

And I would be too.

I couldn't go rogue. Not like Darren had. But there was hope for Darren. That meant there would be hope for me.

Because I didn't want to disappoint Romy, not

after all she had been through. I couldn't hurt her, and therefore I had to stay whole. I had to stay sane.

Darren had a family who loved and relied on him and yet he'd gone rogue. There were stressors that could have turned him, and yet it felt as if something else was going on.

Something we didn't know as a Pack, but would have to unravel. Something was creating rogues, or at least allowing them to come to fruition. That meant our Pack as well as the Talons needed to ensure that we didn't lose anyone else.

I had to hope we would find a way. After all, my twin was working on the problem as we spoke. And I would do all that I could to help her because I needed to stay sane. I needed to be there for my mate.

And as Darren turned back to human and whimpered in Kade's arms, I knew that we all needed to find a way.

Something was coming. We all knew that. We just couldn't be too late.

Mark began to work on my wound as Romy wrapped her arms around me, holding me close.

I had found my mate, and as the snow began to turn to ice, leeching the warmth from our bodies, I knew we would have to go inside soon. We would have to face the next day, and then the next, knowing that something was out there, something we didn't know how to fight yet.

But we were strong. We were Pack.

And I had my mate.

CHAPTER 8

Romy

THE FOLLOWING day warmed up slightly, but not enough. I had slept in my mate's arms, needing to ensure that he was whole. I couldn't understand how things could happen so quickly. I knew this was the way of wolves, and yet it felt so strange. This is a man I hadn't expected, and yet here he was, in my arms, in his home. We had wanted Conner to be near his Pack in case the wound worsened, but his Healer was good, and the strength of his Alpha meant that Mark could pull on those bonds if needed.

That all meant that my mate was pretty much healed and just needed rest.

The other Pack members had taken Darren away to heal, much like the other rogue that they had caught only a few weeks ago.

We had more rogues than ever, wolves that couldn't hold on to their own power, strength, and humanity.

But we were also saving more than ever. I had to hope that there was something in that. That somehow, we were finding a way to make it work.

We would find what was changing them, what was sending them over the edge, but for now, I would focus on what we had.

Conner's home was slightly bigger than mine, full of memories and hope. There were pictures on the wall of his large family. There were memories and tokens from his thirty years of life strewn about the place.

He was so much younger than me, but in the ways of wolves, perhaps in the way that he lived, was older than I was. I had dealt with pain after pain and then hidden myself for decades, but he had found a way to thrive even on the fear of what he might become because of the strength of his wolf. He still fought. He still lived.

His home was a *home*. His bed was soft, a large king easily big enough for two. There was a guest room and an office, and there were places to grow. He had land, and the home didn't set off feelings of despair and loneliness.

I didn't know what our future held, but I knew I never wanted to sleep under my roof again. Maybe I could move in here, in the Redwood den, even though I was a Talon. After all, others did it now. Our dens were so connected it didn't matter that there were miles between us. We found ways to make it work.

Our Pack was becoming one.

Our den would be doing the same.

"You're thinking too hard. It's hard for me to sleep."

I smiled down at him.

"Oh?"

"I'm just saying. You make it difficult."

"I'm just thinking about where I want to wake up tomorrow. And the next day. And the next." He looked up at me, and I grinned down at him. He lay on his back in his bed, naked and hard.

He was fully healed and fully erect.

I grinned at that and looked down at the clothes I still wore. He had shifted to wolf and back to finish the healing process and hadn't bothered with clothes. I had slept nearly on top of him in my clothes, warm and happy, but not wanting to get naked and have ourselves fall into bed with one another when he was still healing. And yet, he was healed, and I wanted more.

"Stay," he said as he reached up and cupped my face. "Stay here with me."

My heart ached even as it swelled three sizes along the mating bond. "Although your home is already a *home,* it feels just like you. And I wouldn't mind finding a way to make it my own with you. Make it us."

"Change anything that you want, make anything that you want. I want to figure out who we are together. I want this. I can go to the Talons if you want, we can make a den there. You just let me know."

I shook my head as I leaned down and captured his lips. "No, the Talons are my Pack, and I need them, but your family is here. Your large, wild, amazing family is here. I want to get to know them. To be close. I've not been close with family in a long time. We'll find a way to make it work, have my duties be between both dens or something. I'm sure

Gideon and Kade already have a plan. That seems like our Alphas."

"I'm sure they do. And later, we can finish planning their event for them. We can plan what we need to do to make this place ours, but for now, I want you, Romy."

"I choose you, Conner." I smiled as I said it, and his wolf pushed at me as my wolf danced around the bond, prancing as if she had never been loved before.

Our wolves had chosen each other before the humans had a chance, and this man beneath me, with his strength and his growly nature, showed me that this was what I wanted, what I had been missing. And I never wanted to let go. I reached between us, under the covers, and gripped him. He groaned, his eyes glowing gold as I stroked him softly.

"Is this how you're going to wake me up every morning, mate of mine?"

"Maybe I can try something else, to see. We don't want to get complacent after all." I lowered myself down, wiggling lower on the bed, and he groaned when I moved the blanket, hovering over his cock. He was thick, long, and far too big for me, but I didn't care. I gripped the base of him before I slowly lapped at the tip of his dick, swallowing the whole of him in my mouth. His hand slid through my hair, gripping tightly as I hollowed my mouth and began to go down on him. The musky scent nearly sent me over the edge, and I kept licking, sucking, loving the way he moved. It was slow, a wake-up, sensuality in its essence.

And when I pulled away and licked my lips, he groaned. "I need you."

"Same."

I stripped off my clothes quickly and hovered over him. With one hand on his shoulder, the other around his cock, I slowly positioned myself over him and sank down. We both let out a hiss of breath as he stretched me, and then I rocked, gripping his hands as we melded together.

"You're so beautiful," he whispered.

"I could say the same for you, but I don't want to make you think I don't think you're all manly and Alpha-y."

"Don't you worry. My dick's inside you right now. I think we can make do."

I laughed, not aware I could laugh at this moment, but it didn't matter.

This is who I had been missing, what I had been missing this entire time, and this was all that mattered. We moved slow, learning one another. Figuring out what made each other breathe faster or slow down. Everything was a discovery, a pleasure, a way to find one another, and when he rolled us both on our sides, and I lifted one leg over his hip, he pushed into me harder, faster. We clung on to one another, my claws going down his back, his on my hip. And when he pulled out again, slid me onto my stomach, and pounded into me from behind, I moved into him, breath for breath, move for move. And then his fangs slid into my shoulder, and I groaned, my mate, marking me as his. Our wolves had already done that, in essence, through a bond, but now it was true. It was our choice. He lapped at the wound and then pulled out of me again before turning me back on my back. I opened my legs for him, welcoming him deep inside me as I came, not once, not twice, but three times. He pounded into me hard, both of us shaking from release, and then he tilted his head to the side, and I finally bit down, marking him as mine. My wolf howled in triumph, knowing I had finally made a choice that she had made days ago.

This man was ours, forever and on to ever. And when he filled me, coming hard with my name on his lips, both of us called out into the ways of our wolves, marked as one, chosen as one.

I knew then I had been fated for something else,

that my life couldn't be the darkness that I had wrapped myself in so tightly.

I had been fated with this man at one point in my life, but I hadn't realized that this could be it. That this could be what I had been missing all this time. I was no longer hiding. I would find out who I was and what path I needed to take, but I wouldn't be alone.

I had my mate. My salvation, the man I hadn't realized I had needed.

And when he kissed me again, I smiled.

I was turning a hundred years old in less than a week's time.

And yet, it felt like I had been reborn into a new life I was finally prepared for. Into a life I would not have to walk alone.

I found my mate, and this was only the beginning.

CHAPTER 9

Conner

"HAPPY BIRTHDAY," I whispered to my mate as she looked up at me, her eyes slightly wild, her hair disheveled. Her hair had been in a slight wave when she had gotten ready next to me in my bathroom that morning. Both of us were learning our routines while we prepped for the day and the event. However, between my hands through her hair and then hers through it from stress, she had lost some of the work she put into it. I didn't mind. She looked sexy as hell no matter what she wore or how she wore it. Not that she was going to let me say that just then, because I had a feeling she was going to growl at me if I touched her again. At least while we were trying to finish everything up.

"Don't look at me," she growled.

"What do you mean?"

"I am trying to set up for the event, and you keep touching me and making out with me and pulling me into secret corners."

I snorted and reached for her.

"Don't you dare, Conner Jameson!"

"Are you messing with your mate?" Kaylee asked as she came towards me. I opened my arms, my smile wide as I looked over at my twin. Kaylee grinned and wrapped her arms around my waist. I inhaled that familiar scent that was all twin and baby sister wrapped into one and grinned down at her.

"Yes, I am. Now, where's yours?"

She waved her hand over at the new member of the Redwood Pack, as Jason whispered with one of our other siblings.

I shook my head and looked back at my twin. "How the hell did we end up mating at the same time?"

"I have no idea. At least it wasn't like the same hour or anything. Was it?"

"That would be a fun to find out, though," Romy

said as she came to my side. She hugged Kaylee hard, the smile on her face wide and true. For a woman who had no family, she was suddenly surrounded by Jamesons, and honestly, I didn't think Romy minded. With any other person, I would be afraid that we would be too much for her. We tended to do that when it came to other people. Not just with my immediate family, but with all of my cousins and the fact that my uncle was the Alpha, we were intimidating. And yet, Jason and Romy had fit in as if they were always meant to be here. But that was the thing with mates. They *were* always meant to be here.

At that moment, a stampede of wolf pups barreled by on their way to one of the twenty Yule and Christmas trees surrounding the neutral circle. I held back a grin at the antics, then leaned into Romy at her quiet sigh. Eleven baby wolves in wolf form pranced and danced around the adults, letting out little coos and tiny yips. It was so disgustingly cute, even my growly and badass brothers smiled at the sight.

One day I'd have a pup with Romy like that.

One day soon, if I had anything to say about it.

"Are you ready to introduce everyone, big brother?" Kaylee asked as she rolled her eyes.

"You only call me big brother when I'm about to do something I don't want to do."

"Don't worry, I'll be by your side, or at least somewhat behind you, hiding," Romy mumbled, and I held back a grin.

"You're going to be hiding then?" I asked softly as I leaned down and took her lips with mine.

"We have been planning this for nearly a month, and I just want to get it over with."

"Aw, look at you two, birthdays, a Yule party, and new matings, it's like we're all adults or something."

I rolled my eyes and pushed at my sister just slightly so she staggered into her mate's welcoming arms. Jason glared at me, even though his eyes were filled with laughter.

"Stop manhandling my mate."

"Once you learn to growl, pup, we can talk," I teased back, and Kaylee rolled her eyes.

"Welcome to the Pack. We're fun," she said.

"I'm not worried," Jason said, and I could tell he wasn't. He might not have been born a wolf, but he was learning.

Romy took my hand as the Betas of both Packs gave us slight nods.

We were in the neutral territory between the dens, and today was a Yule party for both Alphas.

However, there were more than two Alphas in attendance. Not that I had been aware of that until we had started planning and I'd realized what we needed to do.

Riaz, the Alpha of the Starlight Pack, had come up with Kaylee and Jason to speak with the Alphas. Alistair, the Alpha of the Thames Pack, was actually in the country rather than over in England with his Pack for the holiday. I didn't know why he was here, but apparently it was for his own reasons.

Cole, the Central Alpha, and Chase, the new Aspen Pack Alpha, were here as well, and would be for the beginning of the parties before they went back to their dens with their Packs.

We were all learning how to work with the new Alphas as they settled into their positions. The fact that we were all slowly figuring out who we were was a nice change to the wars we had been in for so long.

Romy tugged me up to the stage as I cleared my throat, and people stopped talking to look at us. I had never had so many wolves facing me before, and my wolf didn't mind it, but I had a feeling that Romy's was only going to last for so long. She might be dominant, but she wasn't a fan of being the center of attention. However, she didn't stand behind me. Instead, she stood at my side, and I looked down at my wolf, the woman who turned one century today. I couldn't help but grin.

"Welcome everyone to our first official dual Yule party."

Everybody cheered, and I shook my head, wondering how the hell I was in charge of this.

"And welcome to our Alphas. All of you," Romy said, and I knew she wasn't just speaking to ours, who were just now coming over the bridge. They had been told just twenty minutes ago what was happening, so that way they wouldn't be in too shocked in front of others. More so that way they knew it was a gift, without feeling weak at all. The subtle differences in figuring out the balance in surprising an Alpha weren't easy, and I hoped we hadn't messed up.

"To say thank you to our Alphas, to our Pack, and to remind everyone that it is the holiday season, and no matter what holiday that you celebrate, we are here for you, and we are glad to celebrate and rejoice together as one."

I looked down at my mate as she spoke and smiled. "And, happy birthday."

She blushed as every single wolf, cat, witch, and human in front of us began to sing to her. She put her hands over her face before she glared between her fingers at me. When Mitchell and his mate showed up with a cake for Romy to blow candles out, she glared at me.

"Did you know this?"

I shook my head, laughter bubbling in my chest. "I didn't. I promise. I would never face your wrath for surprising you like this."

"No, that was all me," Mitchell said as he winked. The fact that the scarred man would wink at me was a little disconcerting. He could break me with his pinky. That was a damn dominant wolf.

I pulled Romy off to the side as Kade and Gideon came up to the stage to give speeches, to speak to the Packs, and welcome everybody for a Yule to be remembered. And when Chase, Cole, Alistair, and Riaz came to the stage, everyone knew this meant something. We were there, as a force of one, against whatever was coming at us. We didn't know what was in the darkness, what would come next, but we were forming alliances and finding who we were as Packs, wolves, as all shifter types.

We were finding our balance.

I was with my mate, my family, and we had a future.

Romy was not forgotten. She was not hidden,

every single person here knew who she was now, and she would never be forgotten again.

This was our life. This was my Romy. I looked at the Alphas, at the Packs that were so interwoven that our bonds were becoming centered as one. I knew that this was our future. We were fated in winter, fated in prophecy, and fated in a forever that wasn't ending anytime soon.

A NOTE FROM CARRIE ANN RYAN

Thank you so much for reading **Fated in Winter!** I LOVE writing this bonus romance. When I wrote Trinity Bound over ten years ago, I never thought I'd write the next generations' romance! I'm thrilled to be writing the Talon Pack series again! And next in the shifter world? I'm heading to the Aspen Pack with Etched in Honor! A certain cat shifter is waiting for her HEA!

The Talon Pack:
Book 1: Tattered Loyalties
Book 2: An Alpha's Choice
Book 3: Mated in Mist

Book 4: Wolf Betrayed

Book 5: Fractured Silence

Book 6: Destiny Disgraced

Book 7: Eternal Mourning

Book 8: Strength Enduring

Book 9: Forever Broken

Book 10: Mated in Darkness

The Aspen Pack Series:

Book 1: Etched in Honor

While you wait for more wolves, try the Ravenwood Coven series!

The Ravenwood Coven Series:

Book 1: Dawn Unearthed

Book 2: Dusk Unveiled

Book 3: Evernight Unleashed

If you want to make sure you know what's coming next from me, you can sign up for my newsletter at www.CarrieAnnRyan.com; follow me on twitter at @CarrieAnnRyan, or like my Facebook page. I also have a Facebook Fan Club where we have trivia, chats, and other goodies. You guys are the reason I get to do what I do and I thank you.

Make sure you're signed up for my MAILING LIST so you can know when the next releases are available as well as find giveaways and FREE READS.

Happy Reading!